For George J. – M.W. For Evie – J. L.

Text copyright © 2004 by Martin Waddell
Illustrations copyright © 2004 by John Lawrence

First U.S. edition 2004

Library of Congress Cataloging-in-Publication Data is available.

Library of Congress Catalog Card Number 2002035004

ISBN 0-7636-2170-6

2 4 6 8 10 9 7 5 3 1

Printed in China

The illustrations in this book were made from vinyl engravings,
watercolor washes, and printed wood textures. The words were made
from an original alphabet engraved in vinyl. Computer technology was
used to bring these hand-crafted elements together.

Candlewick Press
2067 Massachusetts Avenue
Cambridge, Massachusetts 02140

visit us at www.candlewick.com

CANDLEWICK PRESS
CAMBRIDGE, MASSACHUSETTS

Tiny's Big Adventure

MARTIN WADDELL

illustrated by

JOHN LAWRENCE

Two little mice jumped out
of their hole in the barn.
"I want to go to the wheat field,"
Tiny said.
"I'll take you," said his sister, Katy.
Tiny had never been to the
wheat field before.

The two little mice scampered away through the long grass by the side of the stream. They climbed the knobby tree.

They danced along the top bar of the gate.

They ran down the post and . . .

they were in the wheat field.

They played climb-a-stalk and you-can't-catch-me-mouse. Then . . .

"What's that, Katy Mouse?"
Tiny whispered. "Is it a cat?"

"It isn't a cat," Katy said.
"It could be," said Tiny.
"It's a rabbit," Katy said. "I know.
I've seen rabbits before."

They played climb-the-tractor and
sit-on-the-seat. Tiny tried steering,
but the wheel was too big for a
small mouse to turn. Then . . .

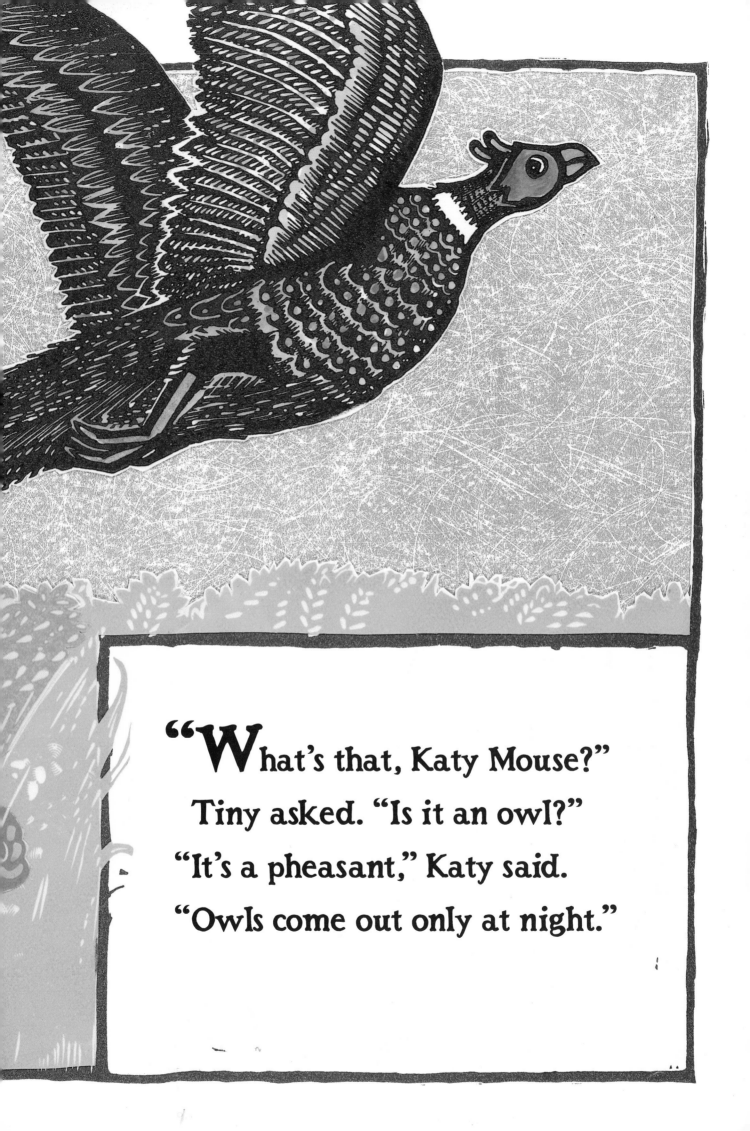

"What's that, Katy Mouse?"
Tiny asked. "Is it an owl?"
"It's a pheasant," Katy said.
"Owls come out only at night."

They started playing again. Tiny
wanted to play hide-and-seek-mouse.
He ran into the wheat field and hid.

Tiny waited and
waited for Katy
to come, but he'd
run too far, and she
couldn't find him.

I'd better
go back,
Tiny
thought.

He ran back
through the
wheat to find
Katy, but . . .

"What's that?"
Tiny said,
and he
quivered.

"What's that?"
Tiny said,
and he
shivered.

"What's THAT?"
Tiny said, and
he shook.
"KATY!"
he called.

And Katy came.

"Thank goodness
I've found you!"
said Katy.
"What are those
scary things,
Katy Mouse?"
sobbed Tiny.

"That's a snail," Katy told him. "Look at his shiny bright shell."

"That's a spider," Katy said. "Look at the sun on her web."

"That's a boot!" Katy told Tiny.

"You were lucky to find it!"

They played little-mouse-house in the boot. They played and they played.

Then the two little mice scampered all the way home.

"That was a big mouse adventure," Tiny said. "Let's do it again, Katy Mouse." And they did.